Ten Sly Piranhas

Ten Sly Piranhas

A Counting Story in Reverse

(A Tale of Wickedness—and Worse!)

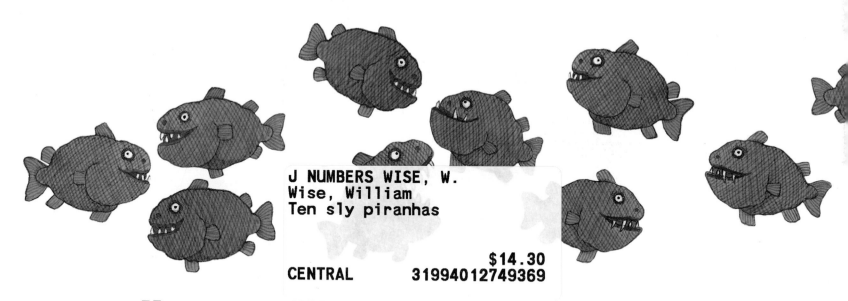

William Wise   pictures by **Victoria Chess**

PUFFIN BOOKS

PUFFIN BOOKS
Published by Penguin Group
Penguin Young Readers Group,
345 Hudson Street, New York, New York 10014, U.S.A.
Penguin Books Ltd, 80 Strand, London WC2R ORL, England
Penguin Books Australia Ltd, 250 Camberwell Road, Camberwell, Victoria 3124, Australia
Penguin Books Canada Ltd, 10 Alcorn Avenue, Toronto, Ontario, Canada M4V 3B2
Penguin Books (N.Z.) Ltd, 182-190 Wairau Road, Auckland 10, New Zealand

First published in the United States of America by Dial Books for Young Readers, a division of Penguin Young Readers Group, 1993
Published by Puffin Books, a division of Penguin Young Readers Group, 2004

1 3 5 7 9 10 8 6 4 2

THE LIBRARY OF CONGRESS HAS CATALOGED THE DIAL EDITION AS FOLLOWS:
Wise, William, 1923–
Ten sly piranhas: a counting story in reverse, a tale of wickedness—and worse!
by William Wise; pictures by Victoria Chess
p. cm.
Summary: A school of ten sly piranhas gradually dwindles as they waylay and eat each other.
ISBN: 0-8037-1200-6 (hc)
[1. Piranhas—Fiction. 2. Counting—Fiction. 3. Stories in rhyme.]
I. Chess, Victoria, ill. II. Title.
PZ8.3.W743 1993 [E]—dc20 91-33704 CIP AC

Puffin Books ISBN 0-14-240074-2

Manufactured in China

For Jack and Eleanor,

who have lived among the real piranhas   W. W.

To Coco and Kyra with much love   V. C.

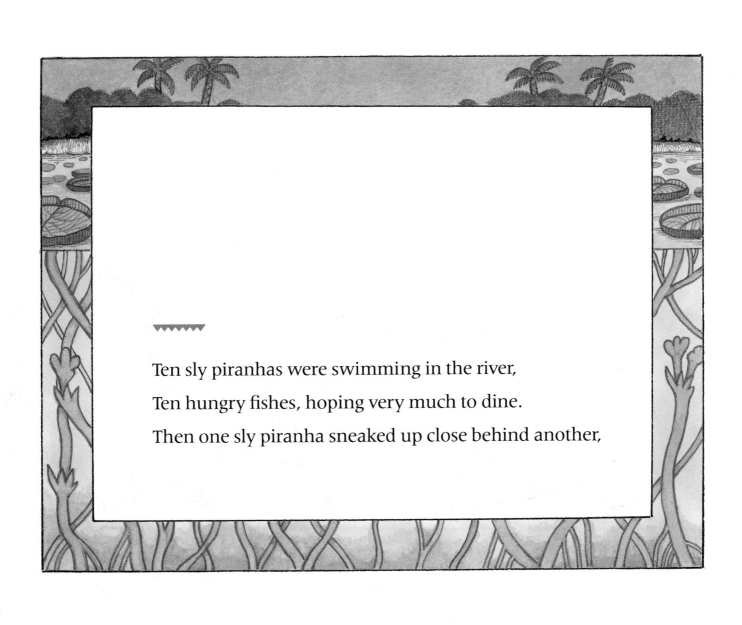

Ten sly piranhas were swimming in the river,

Ten hungry fishes, hoping very much to dine.

Then one sly piranha sneaked up close behind another,

And with a gulp, and a gurgle—

there were only nine.

Nine sly piranhas were swimming in the river,

Nine little tricksters, who were lying there in wait.

Then one said, "My dear, you can trust me like a brother!"

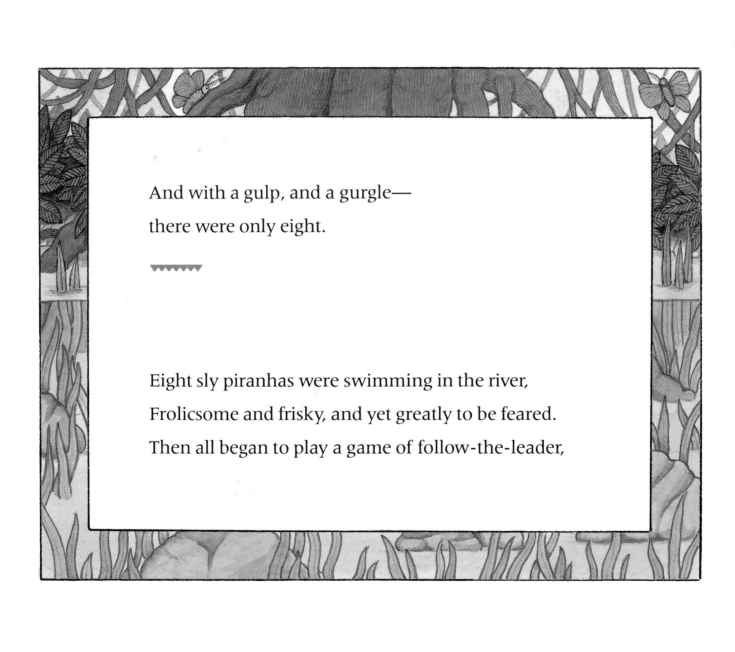

And with a gulp, and a gurgle—

there were only eight.

Eight sly piranhas were swimming in the river,

Frolicsome and frisky, and yet greatly to be feared.

Then all began to play a game of follow-the-leader,

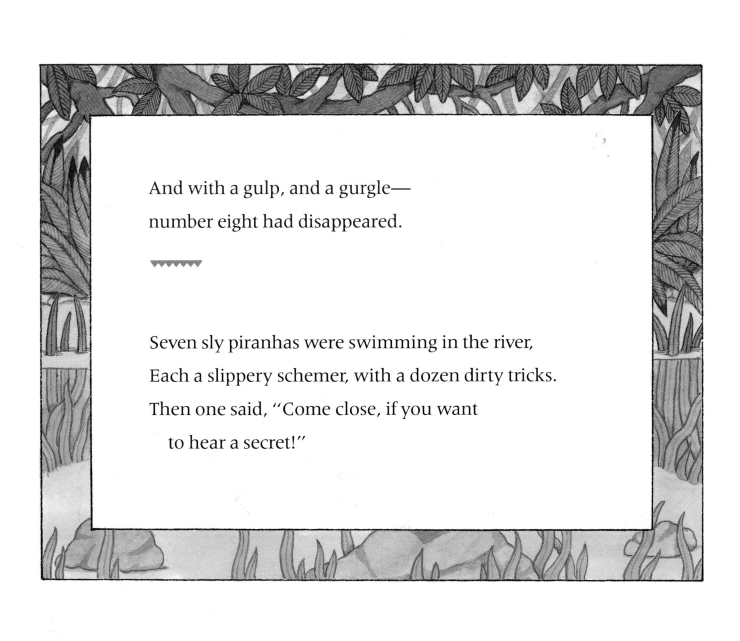

And with a gulp, and a gurgle—

number eight had disappeared.

Seven sly piranhas were swimming in the river,

Each a slippery schemer, with a dozen dirty tricks.

Then one said, "Come close, if you want

to hear a secret!"

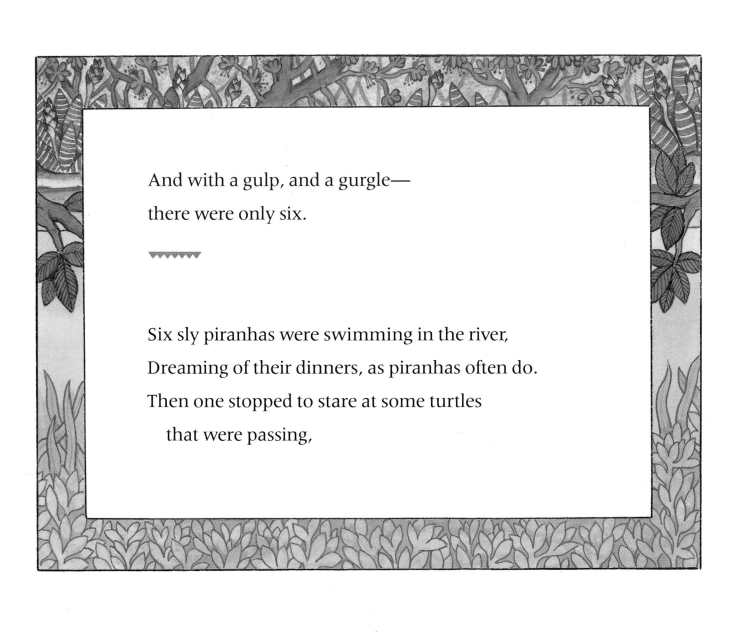

And with a gulp, and a gurgle—

there were only six.

Six sly piranhas were swimming in the river,

Dreaming of their dinners, as piranhas often do.

Then one stopped to stare at some turtles

that were passing,

And with a gulp, and a gurgle—
number six had vanished too.

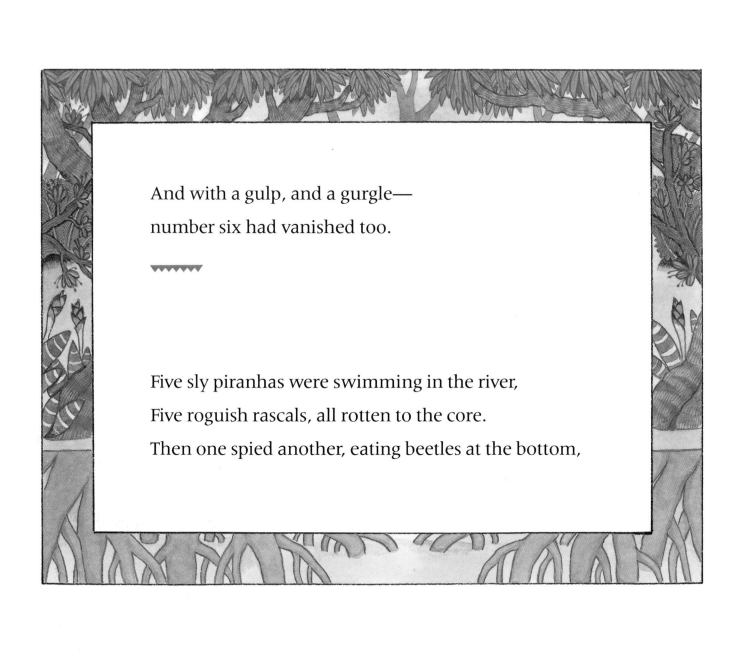

Five sly piranhas were swimming in the river,
Five roguish rascals, all rotten to the core.
Then one spied another, eating beetles at the bottom,

And with a gulp, and a gurgle—

there were only four.

Four sly piranhas were swimming in the river,

Four cool connivers, each as crafty as could be.

Then one found a cave, and asked,

   "Shall we go exploring?"

And with a gulp, and a gurgle—

there were only three.

Three sly piranhas were swimming in the river,

The last remaining members of that memorable crew.

Then one saw his neighbor growing sleepy

in the sunlight,

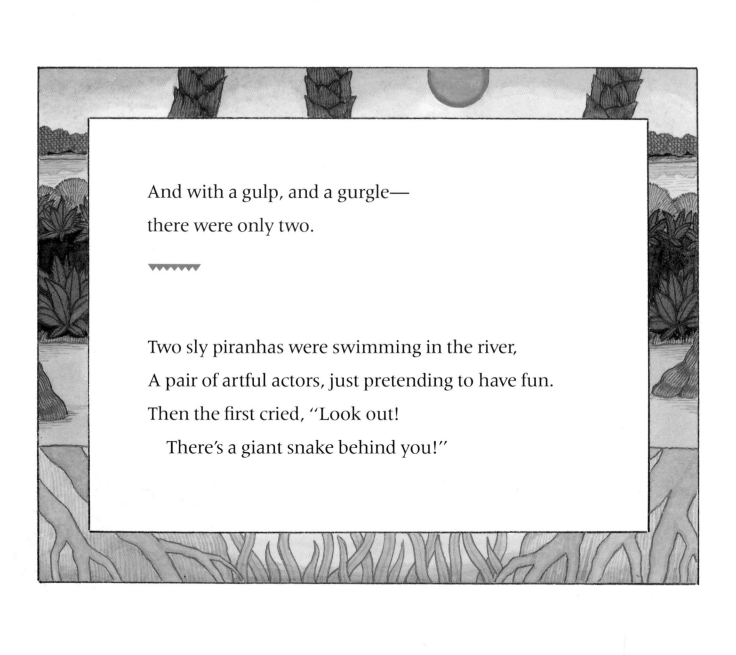

And with a gulp, and a gurgle—

there were only two.

〰〰〰

Two sly piranhas were swimming in the river,

A pair of artful actors, just pretending to have fun.

Then the first cried, "Look out!

There's a giant snake behind you!"

And with a gulp, and a gurgle—

there was only one.

⋁⋁⋁⋁⋁

A single sly piranha was swimming in the river,

More cunning than the others,

for he'd vanquished every one.

Thought he'd grown so clever,

he could eat up *any*body,

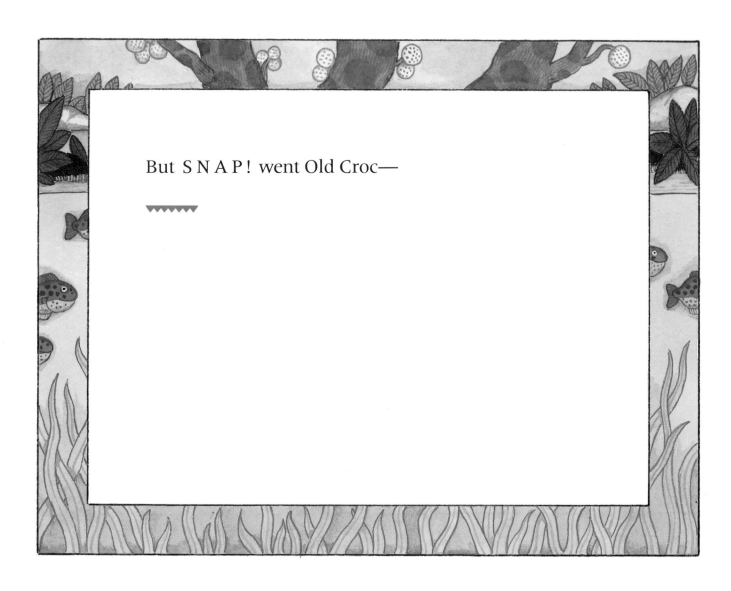

But S N A P ! went Old Croc—

and then there were none.

No sly piranhas were swimming in the river,
Where not so long ago there'd been eight—nine—ten.
And so ends the story of those foxy little fishes—

Unless you'd like to hear it told the same way again.

A NOTE ABOUT PIRANHAS

▼▼▼▼▼▼

Piranhas, also known as caribes, have iridescent scales and can grow up to a foot in length. They travel in tight schools in South American rivers, notably the Amazon. With their powerful jaws and razor-sharp triangular teeth, piranhas can attack cattle and people, though they usually eat other fish instead. And on occasion—"with a gulp, and a gurgle"—they do indeed feed on one another.